Cinderella

A Classic Tale

Retold by
Dr. Alvin Granowsky

Illustrated by
Barbara Kiwak

RAINTREE
STECK-VAUGHN
PUBLISHERS

A Harcourt Company

Austin · New York
www.steck-vaughn.com

Long ago there lived a fine, old gentleman whose
beloved wife died after many happy years of marriage.
The kind man was left alone to raise their sweet and fair
daughter, Ella. He also had to attend to the many details
of keeping a large home. The new duties overwhelmed
the poor man. After a time, Ella's father decided to marry
again. His second wife was a widow with two very
unpleasant daughters, Anastasia and Drusilla. The girls
were proud, vain, and snobbish. People noted how much
they were like their mother.

From their first meeting, the stepmother and her
daughters hated Ella, for she was all that they were not.
Ella was as beautiful inside as out, and the stepsisters
were green with envy. As long as Ella's father was alive,
though, they dared not act on their evil feelings. Sadly,
Ella's father soon died.

After her father's death, sweet Ella was left alone and
unprotected from the wrath of the three selfish women.
They quickly turned Ella into a servant in her own home.
From dawn to dusk, she was put to work. She scrubbed
the floors, scoured the pots, and swept the ashes from the
hearth. While Ella worked, her stepmother and stepsisters
did nothing but urge her to do more.

At night, each stepsister slept on a fine mattress of goose down. Ella slept on a pile of straw laid beside the fireplace. Yet the lovely child endured her new station without complaint. In the rare moments she was allowed to rest, poor Ella would sit in the chimney corner and dream about another world in which life might be sweeter.

It was her habit of finding peace among the cinders that gave Ella's stepsisters cause to mock her with a new name. One evening Drusilla saw Ella daydreaming among the cinders, her face and hair smudged with grime. Despite the soot, Ella glowed with the beauty that only inner goodness can bring.

Drusilla's heart was filled with envy. "Look at those cinders on Ella!" she said. "Did you ever see so many cinders on one person? We should call her Cinderella!"

From that moment forward, all three of the cruel ladies called her Cinderella and nothing else.

For Cinderella, the days dragged on in this unfortunate manner. Then a great occasion came to pass. The king's only son had come of age. It was time for the prince to select a bride, so a royal ball was arranged. At the ball, the prince would meet the finest ladies in the land. Every young lady hoped that she would be chosen to become the wife of the handsome prince. Each girl dreamed of one day being queen.

The stepsisters hoped the prince would invite them. As they waited, they preened and posed before every mirror in the house. One bright day, there came a knock on the front door. A footman in fine livery presented an invitation bearing the royal seal. The invitation brought with it much excitement.

The household was thrown into turmoil. The stepmother and her daughters did not have a moment to spare. The finest silks and satins had to be ordered and then sewn into lovely gowns and ruffled petticoats. Yards and yards of delicate white lace and bright ribbons had to be attached in just the right places.

Each of the sisters demanded the time and attention of everyone in the household. They squabbled between themselves about who would get to wear which colors and fabrics. They fussed over every detail of their dresses. Each worried that the other would gain some small advantage in the prince's favor. There was nothing that the two girls did not find to argue about. They argued most about who was to have the use of Cinderella's services.

Poor Cinderella was kept busy starching and sewing and ironing from dawn to dusk. Yet no matter how hard she tried, she was never able to please her stepsisters.

At last the night of the grand ball arrived. Cinderella, who had a special gift for style despite the rags she wore, helped her vain stepsisters into their lovely gowns. She tried to appear bright and cheerful, but her heart was heavy with longing. "How I would love to go to the prince's ball," said Cinderella with a sigh.

"You at the ball?" Anastasia asked, her round cheeks puffing out in disdain. "Cinderella wants to go to the prince's ball!" she said to her mother and sister.

Drusilla laughed aloud. "It would surely make everyone laugh to see a scullery maid at the prince's ball," she said.

Sweet Cinderella said nothing, though her stepsisters' words hurt her. Her eyes filled with tears as she watched her stepmother and stepsisters stride to the fine coach that awaited them and then ride off to the grand ball. Cinderella rushed to her chimney corner, sat down among the cinders, and wept bitterly.

As she sat there crying, Cinderella felt a cool breeze. She shivered and looked up, thinking that the door had somehow opened. But it was tightly shut. Then Cinderella saw a light swirl down from the ceiling. The light touched the floor and in a blaze of color, a tiny, old lady with a sweet face appeared before Cinderella.

"You needn't cry anymore, Cinderella, for I am your fairy godmother and I have come to help you. Tell me what it is that you want, and I will make your dreams come true," she said.

Cinderella gazed up with wonder in her eyes at the sweet, little woman. "It is my greatest dream to be able to go to the ball and meet the prince. But that will never happen, I know."

"Oh, but it will happen," said the little lady, smiling brightly. "Dry your eyes, child. Run into the garden and bring back the largest pumpkin you can find. Hurry! The ball is about to begin, and we have no time to spare!"

Cinderella did exactly as she was told. As she placed the pumpkin before her fairy godmother, the little lady tapped it with her wand. In an instant, the pumpkin was changed into a beautiful, golden coach. Cinderella smiled with delight at the spectacle before her.

"Now bring me the mousetrap from the pantry," said the fairy godmother.

Cinderella was too amazed to speak. She simply did as she was told without making a sound. She found that the mousetrap was filled with six young mice.

"Ahhh," sighed her fairy godmother as Cinderella set the trap before her. "These mice will make a fine team of horses." She waved her wand, and six white horses with flowing manes pranced before the coach.

"Now you need a coachman to drive them. See if a rat has been caught in the scullery trap," said her godmother.

Cinderella ran to the scullery and returned with a rat trap containing one fat rat with long, white whiskers.

"What a grand coachman we soon will have," said the godmother. She tapped the rat, and in an instant it became a coachman with twinkling eyes and rosy cheeks. The coachman, wearing the finest velvet uniform, stepped up to the horses and harnessed them to the golden coach.

Cinderella gazed in wonder at the coach. Then she looked down at her rags. "How can I go to the ball dressed as I am?" she asked.

"No one will be dressed more beautifully than you," said her fairy godmother.

With a touch of her wand, she transformed Cinderella into a breathtaking sight. Cinderella's beauty, which shone even when she was covered in soot, was now overwhelming. Cinderella looked like a princess. Her dress shimmered with silver and gold, and the diamond clasp in her hair sparkled like evening stars. On her feet she wore delicate slippers made of glass.

"Now go and be happy as you deserve to be," her fairy godmother said. "But I have a warning for you. Be certain to leave the ball before midnight. When the clock strikes twelve, you will find yourself in rags and the coach, coachman, and horses will be what they were before."

"Never fear!" cried Cinderella, her eyes aglow with happiness. "I shall not forget! Goodbye and thank you!"

The coachman snapped his whip, and the horses leaped forward. Cinderella was on her way to the ball.

Cinderella arrived at the height of the ball. The violins were playing, and a swirl of dancing people in elegant attire colored the ballroom floor. A sudden hush silenced the gathering as all eyes turned to the top of the staircase where the beautiful Cinderella stood.

"Who is she?" the whispers began. "She must be a princess, a grand princess indeed! Why, she is absolutely stunning! Has the prince seen her?"

Suddenly, the prince caught sight of the beautiful, young woman descending the marble staircase. He went to her and extended his hand. "Please, may I have the honor of this dance?" he asked. The prince danced every dance with Cinderella.

Everyone wondered who Cinderella was. Even her stepmother and stepsisters did not recognize her, though she spoke sweetly to them. They all tried to find out the identity of the lovely stranger. But Cinderella was careful to say nothing about herself.

Just before twelve o'clock, she whispered to the prince, "I must leave now."

Before he could beg her to stay, Cinderella was gone.

When her stepmother and stepsisters returned from the ball, Cinderella pretended she had been asleep and greeted them with a yawn. "The ball must have been wonderful," she said.

"It was more than wonderful!" Drusilla exclaimed.

"How sad that you had to miss it," said Anastasia maliciously. "The most beautiful girl was at the ball. Everyone was stunned by her beauty, especially the prince."

"What was her name?" asked Cinderella.

"No one knows, not even the prince. He is having another ball tomorrow night, hoping that she will return," said Drusilla.

At the news that the prince wanted to see her again, Cinderella's heart was filled with joy. "May I go to the ball tomorrow evening?" she asked shyly.

Both stepsisters shrieked in indignation that scullery maids did not belong at the prince's ball. Their mother gave Cinderella a scornful look.

"Of course you may go to the ball," she said mockingly, "if you have a proper gown."

Tears sprang to Cinderella's eyes. She knew that if she even tried to borrow an old dress from her stepsisters, they would simply rip it away from her.

The next day the house was filled with excitement. That night's ball was to be even more elaborate than the first. Though the two stepsisters tried to make themselves as lovely as they could be, their looks could never compare to Cinderella's. All the ribbons, lace, and corsets in the world could not make the stepsisters as beautiful as Cinderella was in her rags.

As the time to depart approached, Cinderella's stepmother called out, "Cinderella, we are leaving now. Finish your work while we enjoy ourselves at the ball."

"It is such a pity that you cannot join us," Drusilla said with a sneer.

"I am sure you would love to see that beautiful princess," said Anastasia. "That is, if she comes back."

As she watched the ladies leave for the ball, Cinderella did indeed wonder if she would be able to go back to the palace. Would she ever see the prince again?

She was ashamed to go to the ball dressed in her rags, but she had no other clothes to wear. Not knowing what else to do, Cinderella slumped into her chimney corner and cried.

Then, just as before, a swirl of light came down from the ceiling. Suddenly the godmother appeared. "Why should you be crying, dear Cinderella, on the night of the prince's ball? Did you think that I had forgotten you?"

Her fairy godmother tapped Cinderella's shoulder with her wand, and the tattered dress became a magnificent gown of satin and silk. She was adorned with emeralds and pearls, and her long, golden tresses were arranged in a beautiful fashion. On her feet she wore delicate slippers made of glass.

Just as the evening before, her fairy godmother turned a pumpkin into a coach, mice into white horses, and a rat into a coachman. As she helped Cinderella into the coach, her fairy godmother cautioned her, "Be certain to leave the ball before midnight. When the clock strikes twelve you will find yourself in rags and the coach, coachman, and horses will be what they were before."

"I will not forget, fairy godmother," said Cinderella.

Again, as on the evening before, Cinderella arrived at the height of the ball's splendor. All eyes turned toward the top of the staircase to see the new arrival.

"The princess has returned!" people whispered. "Why, she is even more stunning than before! That gown is truly magnificent, and those emeralds and pearls are beyond compare! Has the prince seen her yet?"

Just as on the evening before, the prince made his way to the lovely Cinderella. "I was hoping you would return. Please dance with me again," he said.

The prince took Cinderella into his arms, and they danced away the evening. It was clear to all those watching that the handsome prince was taken with the beautiful lady. After her arrival, just as the night before, he danced with no other ladies. The two of them were having a wonderful time. It seemed the hours passed as minutes. Soon the clock chimed the hour of twelve.

All at once, Cinderella realized that she had lost track of time. She broke away from the prince and moved quickly through the crowded dance floor. As she rushed up the marble stairway, one of her slippers caught on a stair. Cinderella had no time to stop and retrieve it. She disappeared into the night, leaving her slipper behind.

Moments later, the confused prince made his way up the staircase looking for the lovely lady. He saw the glass slipper and picked it up. He walked to the door and asked the doorman, "Did you see a beautiful lady in a stunning gown leave the ballroom?"

"No, your royal prince," said the doorman. "I saw only a girl in rags running off into the night."

By morning, the kingdom was alive with talk of the beautiful stranger. The prince was hopelessly in love with her, though he did not know her name. The glass slipper she had left behind was his only hope of finding her. That afternoon, everyone in the kingdom gathered to hear the royal proclamation. All the ladies in the land would have an opportunity to try on the glass slipper. The prince would marry the lady whose foot could fit the slipper.

For days the prince and his footman went from house to house searching the kingdom for the lady who could wear the slipper. Hundreds of ladies tried on the slipper, but it fit none of them.

At last the prince and his footman arrived at Cinderella's home. Cinderella watched from behind a door as first one stepsister and then the other strained to get her foot into the tiny slipper. Though each pulled and tugged to get the slipper on, neither could make it fit.

The footman looked around and asked, "Are there any other ladies in the house?"

"Only a scullery maid," said the stepmother.

The stepsisters laughed aloud at the idea of Cinderella trying on the slipper.

But the prince said, "Allow the maiden to have a turn."

Cinderella shyly stepped forward. Her foot slipped easily into the tiny, glass slipper. Everyone was amazed. Then Cinderella produced the other glass slipper from her pocket and quickly slipped it on as well. A light swirled down from the ceiling, and Cinderella's fairy godmother appeared. With a tap of her wand, she transformed Cinderella into the stunning, young woman who had charmed everyone at the ball.

The prince took Cinderella's hand and knelt before her. "I cannot live without you. Please say you will marry me," he said.

"Yes, I will marry you," Cinderella replied with a smile.

Cinderella's stepmother and stepsisters begged her to forgive them for the years of cruelty they had made her endure. Cinderella forgave them gladly and invited them to visit her at the palace.

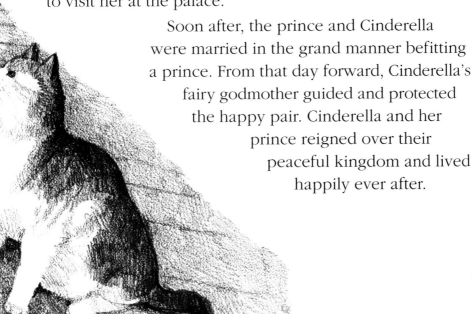

Soon after, the prince and Cinderella were married in the grand manner befitting a prince. From that day forward, Cinderella's fairy godmother guided and protected the happy pair. Cinderella and her prince reigned over their peaceful kingdom and lived happily ever after.

Steck-Vaughn
POINT
of
VIEW
Stories

That *Awful* Cinderella

By
Dr. Alvin Granowsky

Illustrated by
Rhonda Childress

RAINTREE
STECK-VAUGHN
RSVP PUBLISHERS

A Harcourt Company

Austin • New York
www.steck-vaughn.com

Gossip, gossip, and more gossip! That's all you hear around this kingdom nowadays. Ever since that awful Cinderella married the prince, the horrible gossip about us has not ceased. Anastasia and I have been called "wicked stepsisters." Mother has been called a "wicked stepmother." Each day the insults get worse.

Well, if our neighbors want to gossip about something, they should talk about what really happened—to **us**, not to Cinderella. People have the whole story backwards. They say we were unkind to Cinderella. Ha! and another ha! We weren't unkind to that girl. We gave her a place to live, didn't we? Keeping Cinderella around was Mother's idea. Personally, I have never believed in handouts. I look out for myself, and I expect others to do the same. I mean, let's face facts! After Cinderella's father died, there was no earthly reason for her to stay with us. She belonged at the orphanage down the road, and that's what Anastasia and I often told Mother. Mother raised us to be honest— to respect the truth, you know. So we state things as they are—no mealy-mouthed mincing of words for us.

Unfortunately, people don't always appreciate honesty. They'd rather hear what they want to hear. Still, I always say what I think. And I said what I thought about Cinderella.

"That girl is awful, just awful," I would say to Mother. "Why do you allow her to stay here? Those filthy rags she wears are so depressing! They have an odor! Her hair is tangled and stringy! And she never takes a bath."

Anastasia agreed completely, but Mother always looked on the bright side. She was kind to a fault. "After all," she would say, "I was married to the girl's father. He left us the gold and silver that we need in order to live like ladies. It just wouldn't look right to throw his only child out on the street."

"Why are you being so foolish?" we would ask. "Do you think for a moment that that awful Cinderella would hesitate to throw us out if she were in our shoes?"

Mother would smile and say, "As long as she remembers to stay in her place and be grateful for what we give her, can't we try to tolerate the pitiful child? If nothing else, she does the chores. We must have **someone** to clean the house and wash our clothes. In honor of her father's memory, and all the worldly goods he left us, I would like to offer his only child a place to sleep and a way to earn her living. Call it a weakness if you want, but that's the way I feel."

It was a weakness all right. Providing a home for that orphan got us nowhere. In fact, it practically ruined Mother's health. Because of all the gossip, she just stays home, lying in bed with a cool rag on her forehead. The woman is suffering! Who knows if Mother will ever recover? That's what happens to people who are naive enough to devote their life to caring for those who don't take care of themselves.

Cinderella could have taken care of herself. She just didn't want to. She preferred to let us take care of her. When I think of how that hateful girl took advantage of my family's kindness and then did us all in, ME in particular, I could just scream!

Now let me tell you exactly what happened and how it happened. I'll give just the facts uncolored by emotion. Then you can decide for yourself who mistreated whom. That awful Cinderella! When I think of what happened, I would like to spit on her shoes and rip her gown!

You see, we got an invitation to the prince's ball that said all ladies were invited. Well, naturally, that meant my sister Anastasia and me. But Cinderella is such a grabby girl, she pulled the invitation from my hand and said she was invited too. Ha! and another ha! That was silly! The prince did not want scullery maids at his party. He wanted lovely ladies, like me.

As busy as we were preparing to look beautiful for the prince's ball, Anastasia and I took valuable time to help Cinderella understand why it was not appropriate for her to be at the ball. "You scrub floors. You carry ashes from the fireplace. You wash dishes and take out garbage. That is what you do because you are a servant. Please take an honest look at yourself so that you see yourself as we see you each day. You wear rags. You are dirty. In fact, you have an odor about you. You need a bath. Clearly, you are not a lady who would be invited to a prince's ball. Do you understand? This invitation is specifically addressed to 'All ladies in the land.' It very clearly is not addressing you!"

Ye are invited to a Royal Ball

You would think that explanation would be enough. But we explained even further to be sure that she understood. "You are not a lady. **We** are ladies. You live here only because our mother is kindhearted to the point of foolishness. Also, we find it useful to have you do our work. Now, return our invitation immediately!"

Cinderella smiled sweetly at those words, as if she were grateful for our guidance. We thought she finally understood. We were taken in by that dishonest girl's act.

She acted like the sweetest thing. Ha! and another ha! She ran here and there helping us prepare for the prince's ball. There was nothing she wouldn't do for us. We should have known that she was up to something.

Why, sugar would have melted in her mouth as she saw us off to the ball. "Dear Drusilla, everyone will be sure to notice you with your hair piled so high on your head," Cinderella said. "Sweet Anastasia, you look wonderful in your gown! No one will ever realize how heavy you are!"

We drove off to the prince's ball, happy and content in the knowledge that we had helped a young girl come to terms with her station in life. Little did we know that while we were on our way to the ball, that awful Cinderella was meeting with her fairy godmother — a vagrant she invited into our home.

Wouldn't it have been the honest thing for her to say, "I fully realize that the prince does not want me at his ball. If he did, the invitation would have stated, 'Servants and scullery maids are invited.' Still, in spite of knowing that I am definitely not wanted and do not belong at the ball, I plan to go."

Cinderella should have said, "My fairy godmother will arrive soon and make me look like a princess. She will cast a spell to make the prince fall in love with me. I know that isn't fair, but then, that is not my concern. My only concern is to marry the prince and make you miserable."

If she had told us her plan I could have respected her honesty. But she did no such thing.

We arrived at the ball late so that we could make a grand entrance. And I must say, when we walked down that marble staircase together, no one could take their eyes off us. I mean, there was Anastasia, who is one of the homeliest girls in the kingdom, standing next to me, the most beautiful. Naturally, people would think, "How did that homely girl get such a beautiful sister?"

Then Anastasia tried to shove me down the stairs, and I'm sure they all understood how she felt. Really, how would you feel if you were fat and homely and had a tall, slim, beautiful girl like me for a sister? When I kicked Anastasia in the shins, I know everyone thought, "It is a good thing that beautiful girl can take care of herself!"

Then the prince entered the ballroom. And he saw me! Our eyes met! And then he shook his head because he was dazzled by my beauty. My striking beauty stunned him so much that he had to turn his back to me. He would have fainted dead away if he hadn't.

Then just as he was about to turn back around to ask me to marry him, Cinderella entered the ballroom. I did not know it was Cinderella, of course, or I would have told everyone that she was a scullery maid with no right to impose herself on this crowd of courtly people.

Well, the prince took one look at Cinderella and forgot all about me. You see, Cinderella's fairy godmother had cast a despicable spell on my prince to make him fall in love with Cinderella. It was so unfair! Should I lose the prince just because I don't have a fairy godmother?

Anyway, the prince danced with Cinderella all evening. And everyone asked who that beautiful girl was. Even Anastasia! Poor Anastasia. She's the homeliest girl in the kingdom, and she's not so smart, either.

When we came home from the ball that night, Anastasia couldn't quit rattling on about that bee-ooo-ti-ful girl who had enchanted the prince. I'm afraid my breaking heart took over and I screamed, "Anastasia, it's bad enough I have to look at your homely face. Must I also listen to your stupid talk?"

But Cinderella was fascinated by Anastasia's chatter. After all, it was about her. "Oh, was she really that beautiful?" Cinderella asked. "Did the prince really dance with only her all evening? You say he is having another ball tomorrow night so she'll come back again?"

Try to explain away that bit of play-acting on her part. Just to be kind, we shared all the details of our eventful evening, and the whole time that nasty, little girl was planning to use the information to do us in.

Mother was totally taken in by Cinderella's excitement about the ball. Mother is just so gullible sometimes. She fell for Cinderella's act and felt sorry for her. She told Cinderella she could come with us to the ball the next evening if she could get herself a gown. When Anastasia and I heard that, we just screamed.

Mother said not to worry because in the end everything would turn out right. Ha! and another ha! That just goes to show you how wrong our softhearted mother can be!

The next evening I looked beautiful. I had a new hairdo that was just right for my beautiful face and my gown was perfectly tailored for my wonderful figure. Why, Mother said she had never seen such beauty! And Anastasia, who I know is jealous of me because I am so beautiful, could hardly think of any nasty things to say about me.

Just as we were about to leave the house, Cinderella charged at us and yelled at the top of her lungs, "Wait! Wait for me!"

There she was, running after us in a gown that looked very familiar. Well, Anastasia and I took one look at her and screamed. The nerve of that girl! All our guidance about why it was not appropriate for a scullery maid to go to the prince's ball had gone in one ear and out the other!

She had not paid us the least mind. Cinderella was dressed for the ball in a gown made from some of our best, old rags! She hadn't asked permission to use our rags! Really! What was she thinking? What would she use to polish the furniture if she used all the best rags to make a dress? Naturally, Anastasia and I just took our rags right back again! And rightfully so. They were ours, weren't they? After stealing our rags, that awful Cinderella had the nerve to fall down on the floor and start crying about how mean we were to her!

Mother, Anastasia, and I went off to the ball. We thought we did not have to worry about Cinderella again that evening. But what a mistake that was! While we were driving to the ball, she was meeting with that fairy godmother again. Soon my dreams of lifelong happiness with the prince would be destroyed—all because of that awful Cinderella.

At the ball I spent the evening trying to make the prince's eyes meet mine again. I wanted to set his heart afire with thoughts of what was meant to be. But that didn't happen because Cinderella's fairy godmother had cast a despicable spell on my prince. The poor man just could not take his eyes off Cinderella because of that stupid spell. Of course, we didn't know it was Cinderella who was hogging the prince. If we had known, we would have put that scullery maid in her place. But we didn't know, so all we could do was watch the two of them.

Then the clock struck twelve. Well, I never saw such carrying on! I mean, really, what that selfish brat won't do to get attention! First she came in late to make a grand entrance. And then, after she had stolen all the attention during the ball, she screamed, "Oh, my goodness, the clock is chiming twelve!" Then she rudely left the prince, ran up the stairs, and out of the ballroom. She just disappeared without even a "Thank you for having me," (which I guess is about right, since she wasn't invited anyway).

What a way to get attention! How could anyone think that girl is sweet and innocent? Ha! and double ha! Really, it's too embarrassing the way that Cinderella carried on. What's worse is that that awful girl had the nerve to leave one of her glass slippers behind as if by accident. Some accident! You know perfectly well she did it on purpose. She had it all planned out—she and that fairy godmother. Oh, if only I'd had the least inkling of what was really happening. But how could I have known? I didn't know Cinderella even had a fairy godmother.

The next day we heard that the prince intended to have every lady in the land try on the glass slipper that was left behind at the ball. He would travel throughout the kingdom searching for the girl whose foot could fit into the shoe. He would marry that girl.

Here was my chance! I knew that once the prince saw my lovely face again and looked into my beautiful eyes, he would fall madly in love with me. I could see myself reigning as Princess Drusilla. The prince and I would be so happy living in that great big palace!

I waited for days and days. I had to look my best every minute because I never knew when the prince might show up.

Finally, we heard a knock at the door—the moment I had been waiting for. When Mother opened the door, I was ready to dazzle the prince with my beauty and charm. Just as our eyes were about to meet across the room, Anastasia jumped in front of me.

"Let me try on the slipper first!" cried Anastasia. Really, she acts so terrible, you would never believe we are sisters!

Well, Anastasia plopped right down on the floor and shoved her big, fat foot right into the prince's face. It was just pathetic how that desperate girl tried to stuff her huge foot into that tiny shoe.

The poor prince was just horrified. Naturally Anastasia could not even get her big toe into that tiny, glass slipper.

"Is there another lady in the house?" the prince asked.

"Yes, my prince, I am here!" I said, as I stepped forward. I was so breathtaking that the prince was overwhelmed.

"Do you remember me, my prince?" I whispered. "I am the beautiful lady you saw at the ball."

The prince was speechless. He stared into my eyes. Then he had to turn his back to me, just as he had done at the ball, so he wouldn't faint. That's when I knew things were going my way. My dazzling good looks had enchanted the prince.

"You do remember me, don't you?" I asked softly.

But before the prince could answer, his footman said, "All right, miss, try on the slipper!"

I lifted my slim, beautiful leg, and said, "Slip on the shoe, my handsome prince."

The footman slid the slipper onto my foot. "It fits!" I cried.

"It fits!" the prince cried. He was as happy as I was.

But then that dumb footman saw that my silly, little toe was not in the slipper.

The prince was devastated at the news that the slipper didn't quite fit me after all. He looked so heartbroken. Then I thought of a way to solve the problem of that stupid shoe being just a little too tight.

"Cut off the toe!" I cried. "It means nothing to me! Mother, remove the toe! Quickly!"

Then the prince murmured that it wouldn't be fair to all the other ladies of the land, or something like that. I know it just broke his heart to have to say that.

The footman looked around the room and asked, "Are there any other ladies in the house?"

"No!" we all answered. And that was absolutely true because Cinderella was no lady. She was a scullery maid who was living in our house only because Mother has a soft spot for orphans. But do you think Cinderella admitted she was not a lady and should not be trying on the slipper? Ha! and another ha! Don't make me laugh!

Cinderella leaped in front of the prince and said, "I am a lady and I live in this house."

"Let her try on the slipper," the prince said. "We have searched the whole kingdom, and she is the only lady who has not tried on the slipper."

Who would have believed it? That awful Cinderella stuck out her foot. And of all the terrible things—her foot fit right into the slipper!

That poor prince! He did not know what to say. There he was, madly in love with me, but it was Cinderella's foot that fit into that stupid slipper. What was he to do?

Then that show-off Cinderella pulled the other glass slipper out of her pocket and put it on. The way she was prancing around, you would have thought that stupid shoe was made of gold instead of just plain glass.

And then, while the prince was trying to figure out a way not to marry Cinderella, her fairy godmother appeared and put another rotten spell on him. "I love you Cinderella," the prince said because of the spell. "Be my wife."

Naturally, that awful Cinderella said she would marry the prince. What did she care that she had stolen the man I wanted for my husband? She and that fairy godmother of hers got exactly what they wanted. Cinderella's wedding was a grand affair, which included, of course, a royal ball. I refused to have anything to do with it—I've been to enough royal balls to last me a lifetime. That's where all this trouble started in the first place!

And then of all the nerve, Cinderella invited Mother and Anastasia and me to visit her in the palace! Well, if you think I plan to visit Cinderella in the palace, you must be crazy! Imagine the nerve of that awful girl! If we went to that palace, we would never get out again. She'd like nothing better than to see us as servants there— scrubbing and scouring and sewing.

That awful Cinderella is something else. First of all she is a social climber who took advantage of Mother's generosity. Second, she entered into a plot with her fairy godmother to steal my prince for her husband. And then, as if that were not enough, she invited us to visit her in the palace where she spends her days telling everyone how we abused her and took advantage of her.

Do you know what I say to all of that? Ha! and another ha! Don't make me laugh! I want nothing more to do with that awful Cinderella.